Karen's Snow Day

Look for these
and other books about Karen
in the
Baby-sitters Little Sister series:

Little Sister

Karen's Snow Day

Ann M. Martin

Illustrations by Susan Tang

A
LITTLE APPLE
PAPERBACK

SCHOLASTIC INC.
New York Toronto London Auckland Sydney

ISBN 0-590-45650-4

12 11 10 9 8 7 6 5   6 7 8/9

Printed in the U.S.A.   40

First Scholastic printing, January 1993

For Doug,
a.k.a. my brudda

I Love Snow

"Where is *The Snowy Day*? I want you to read *The Snowy Day*," said Andrew. Andrew is my little brother. He is four going on five.

"Me, too," said Emily Michelle. Emily is my little sister. She is not even three yet. I think "Me, too" are her favorite words.

"Why do you want me to read that book?" I asked. "We do not have any snow. Not one flake."

"I bet we will have some soon," said Andrew. "It feels like snow."

This was true. It was a very wintry Saturday. I was at the big house with Daddy's family, and a fire was blazing in the fireplace. Outside, the sky was gray and the air was icy. It looked like snow, it felt like snow, it even smelled like snow. But Dr. G. the weatherman had not said a word about snow. He had said, "Today will be overcast and chilly, with temperatures in the twenties." That was all. No fair. We are supposed to have snow in the winter. At least we are supposed to have snow here in Stoneybrook, Connecticut.

"Pul-*lease* will you read to us?" begged Andrew.

"You can read by yourself now," I reminded Andrew. (I knew that for a fact. I taught Andrew myself.)

"But I want *you* to read."

"I have an idea," said Kristy. "Let's have a reading party. We will have it by the fire. We will be nice and cozy."

"What is a reading party?" I asked. Kristy is my big sister. She is thirteen. She babysits. And she knows almost everything.

"A reading party is . . ." Kristy paused. I had a feeling she had just made up reading parties this very minute. "It is when everyone gets his favorite book and we all read to each other. If you cannot read, then you just listen."

Well, that sounded like fun. "Who shall we invite?" I asked.

"The whole family," said Kristy.

At Daddy's house, that is a lot of people. Soon ten of us were sitting in the living room: Andrew, Emily, Kristy, and me, plus Daddy, Elizabeth, Nannie, Sam, Charlie, and David Michael. Elizabeth is Daddy's wife. She is my stepmother. Kristy, Sam, Charlie, and David Michael are her kids, so they are my stepsister and stepbrothers. (David Michael is seven like me, but the other boys are older. They are in high school.) Nannie is Elizabeth's mother. This makes her my stepgrandmother. Guess who else came to the reading party. Shannon and Boo-Boo. Shannon is David Mi-

3

chael's puppy. Boo-Boo is a fat old tomcat.

Of course, Andrew brought *The Snowy Day*. Do you know what? He could not read all of it by himself after all. He needed some help. But he read a lot of it.

While he read, I thought about snow. I *love* snow. I love everything about snow. I love watching it and making angels in it and making snowpeople with it.

I was hoping for a snow day. If school closed and I could spend an entire day in the snow, I would be so gigundoly happy!

I was not the only person hoping for snow. Sam and Charlie wanted it, too. They had just bought a used snowblower.

"What for?" asked Andrew.

"To earn money. We can clear people's sidewalks and driveways with it. *If* we ever get any snow," Sam answered.

At the reading party I read some poems from *Now We Are Six*. When I finished, I looked out the window. "I wish it would snow," I said.

"Me, too," said Emily Michelle.

Listening to the Radio

The next day, Sunday, Andrew and I went back to Mommy's house. We got there just in time for dinner. Andrew and I are used to going back and forth between Mommy's house and Daddy's house. We do it pretty often. See, we have two homes.

I am the only person in my second-grade class who lives at two houses. I have two houses and two families, and I call myself Karen Two-Two. This is how I became a two-two.

When I was very little, even younger

than Andrew, I lived in one house with one family — Mommy, Daddy, Andrew, and me. We lived in the big house where Daddy had grown up. Then Mommy and Daddy began to fight. Not just a little. They fought a lot. They said they loved Andrew and me very much, but they did not love each other anymore. And they could not live together. So Mommy moved to another house, a little house. Andrew and I went with her. Then a very surprising thing happened. Mommy and Daddy got married again — but not to each other. Mommy married Seth, and Daddy married Elizabeth. That is how I got my two families.

The little-house family is Mommy and Seth and Andrew and me. Seth is my stepfather. When he moved into our house he brought along his cat and dog. The cat is Rocky and the dog is Midgie. I like Rocky and Midgie very much, except for their names. I think I would have given them prettier names. Guess what. I have a pet of my own at Mommy's. I have a rat. Her name is Emily Junior. (I named her after Emily Michelle.)

Andrew and I spend most of our time at the little house. But every other weekend and on some holidays and vacations, we live with Daddy at the big house. Isn't it lucky the big house is so big? After Elizabeth married Daddy, she moved in with Kristy and Sam and Charlie and David Michael. Then Daddy and Elizabeth adopted Emily Michelle. Emily comes from a country called Vietnam. And *then* Nannie moved in to help take care of Emily. When Andrew and I are at Daddy's house, *ten* people live there. Plus Shannon and Boo-Boo. Oh, and plus Goldfishie and Crystal Light the Second. They are goldfish. They belong to Andrew and me. I named Crystal Light. Isn't that name prettier than Rocky or Midgie?

One day in school, my teacher began to read a book to our class. It was called *Jacob Two-Two Meets the Hooded Fang*. That was when I got the idea to call myself Karen Two-Two. And to call my brother Andrew

Two-Two. We have two of so many things. We have our two houses and two families. We also have two mommies and two daddies, two cats and two dogs. I have two pieces of Tickly, my special blanket. I keep one piece at each house. I have two stuffed cats who look just the same. Moosie stays at the big house, Goosie stays at the little house. I even have two best friends. Hannie Papadakis lives across the street from Daddy and one house down. Nancy Dawes lives next door to Mommy. She is gigundoly lucky because she has a brand-new baby brother. Hannie and Nancy and I are all in Ms. Colman's second-grade class at Stoneybrook Academy. We call ourselves the Three Musketeers.

The night Andrew and I went back to the little house, I decided I better listen to the radio. I wanted some snow to fall. I wanted a snow day when school was closed. Guess what Dr. G. said. He said, "Chance of a light snowfall tonight."

All right! Snow was coming!

All About Snow

On Monday morning when my alarm clock rang, I sat up in bed right away. I wanted to see the snow. I pulled my window shade down, then let it snap up. I peered outside. The ground was white. Dr. G. had been right.

"Snow day! Snow day!" I yelled.

"Karen?" called Mommy from her room. "Are you all right?"

"It snowed!" I shouted. "No school!"

Mommy came into my room. She looked out the window. "It did snow," she agreed.

"But not enough to close school, Karen. Look, the street is only wet. And I think the sun will be out soon."

"But the ground is white," I said. "I better listen to the radio." I turned on my pink sound box. The sound box is very cool. It is a radio and a tape player. Plus, it has a microphone so I can pretend I am a singer on the stage. Usually, I also pretend I have a large audience.

I climbed into bed to listen to the weather report.

"Karen, you need to get dressed," said Mommy. "I promise you will have school. Today is not going to be a snow day."

I did not want to get dressed, but I did it anyway. Also, I listened to the radio. Just in case. Mommy is not *always* right.

I waited for Dr. G. to say, "Stoneybrook Academy is closed." But he did not. He did not say any schools were closed. (Okay, Mommy was right again.)

"Karen, are you dressed?" called Mommy.

10

"Yes!" I replied.

I made my family listen to the radio during breakfast. Still, no schools were closed. Finally Seth said, "Time to go, Karen." He meant time to go to school. I did not mind. I like school.

Nancy and I rode to school together. Seth drove us. When we reached Stoneybrook Academy we ran to Ms. Colman's room. (We are not supposed to run in the halls, but we forget that pretty often.) Hannie was already in our classroom.

"Hi, Hannie!" I called. The Three Musketeers were together again.

Hannie and Nancy and I sat on some desks in the back of the room. We used to sit together all the time. That was before I got glasses. Then Ms. Colman made me move to the front row. Now I sit up there with the other glasses-wearers. They are Natalie Springer and Ricky Torres. Guess what. Ricky and I are pretend married. We had a wedding on the playground one afternoon. So Ricky is my husband.

"Good morning, class!" said Ms. Colman.

Hannie and Nancy and I looked up. Our teacher had come into the room. She clapped her hands. That meant we should sit at our desks and settle down. Time for school to begin.

That morning after reading, Ms. Colman told us to look out the window. "What do you see?" she asked.

I raised my hand. "Snow!" I shouted.

"Yes," replied Ms. Colman. "Thank you, Karen. And please remember to use your indoor voice. We had some snow last night. That is perfect because today we are going to begin a new unit. We will be learning about snow."

I could not believe it. What a great idea. Did Ms. Colman know how much I love snow? Probably. Ms. Colman is the best teacher ever. She is my *favorite* teacher. I just love her. I think she is perfect, even if she does have to tell me to use my indoor voice sometimes.

13

I wished I could invite my teacher over for dinner. That would be so, so cool. None of my teachers has ever been to my house. I decided I would talk to Mommy about my idea right after school.

The Perfect Snow Day

After school, Nancy's mother picked up Nancy and me. Guess who was in the car with her. Danny. Danny is her baby brother. He was in his special car seat, and he was all bundled up. He was wearing so many clothes I could hardly see him.

Nancy sat in front next to her mother. I sat in back next to Danny. I wanted to play with him, but he was asleep. Danny sleeps a lot. He can sleep anywhere.

When Mrs. Dawes parked the car, I said,

15

"Thank you for the ride!" I did not stay to play with Nancy. I did not even stick around to see if Danny would wake up. I just ran to my house. I had to talk to Mommy.

"Mommy!" I called as I dashed through our front door.

"I'm right here," she replied.

Mommy and Andrew were in the living room. Andrew was lining up his little cars along the edge of the rug. Mommy was working at the desk.

"Hi!" I said.

"Hi, honey," said Mommy. "How was school?

"Fine. Can Ms. Colman come over for dinner sometime?"

"What?" said Mommy.

"Your *teacher*?" said Andrew.

"Yes, my teacher. Can she come over for dinner?"

"Oh, Karen, I don't know," said Mommy.

"Please? I bet she would love to come."

16

"I do not want to bother her," said Mommy.

"Dinner would not bother her," I said.

"We will see," said Mommy. "Let me think about it."

When Mommy says "We will see," she means stop asking questions. So I went to my room and turned on my sound box. It was time to listen to the radio some more. While I listened, I played with Emily Junior. I let her crawl around in my closet and look for hiding places. Then I put her back in her cage. I was telling her the story of the Twelve Dancing Princesses when I heard the announcer say, "Now here is Doctor G. with the weather."

"Just a sec," I said to Emily. I listened carefully.

"Expect more light snow tomorrow night," said Dr. G.

"Yes!" I cried. "Emily, I will finish that story later."

I ran for the phone. I called Nancy. "Come over, okay?" I said.

Nancy came right over. "Doctor G. says we will have more snow tomorrow," I told her. "More snow already."

"A blizzard?" asked Nancy. (Nancy wanted a snow day, too.)

"Not a blizzard," I admitted. "But maybe we will have one soon. It snowed last night, and now it is going to snow again. This must be snow season. It is probably time to get ready for a snow day."

"I am ready now," said Nancy. "My radio is turned to Doctor G."

"But we should make plans," I said. "We should plan the perfect snow day."

"Let's call Hannie," said Nancy. "We have to plan it with her."

We used the phone in the kitchen. I found a pad of paper and a pencil so I could write down ideas. When Hannie was on the phone, I said, "What should we do on a snow day?"

"Drink hot chocolate with marshmallows," said Hannie.

"Go sledding," said Nancy.

18

I made a list on the pad. Then I added *Go skating*.

"Put down 'Build a snowman,' " said Hannie.

"And 'Make snow angels,' " said Hannie.

When our list was finished, it was pretty long. We would be busy on our snow day. And we would have gigundo fun.

It's a Deal!

Before we knew it, Andrew and I were back at the big house for another weekend. And snow was on the ground.

"Karen," said Andrew after dinner on Friday night. "You could have your snow day tomorrow. I think maybe there is enough snow to make a snowman. And I have already made snow angels."

"Oh, Andrew," I said. He is just too little to understand some things. "A snow day is not just *any* day. It is a day when school is closed. So it cannot be a Saturday. And a snow day is the day after a snowstorm. It is not supposed to snow tonight. So tomorrow will not be a snow day."

"Oh. I'm sorry," said Andrew.

"That is okay. You'll learn." I hugged my brother.

Andrew was right about one thing, though. We did have enough snow to make a snowman and snow angels. Every few days, a little more snow fell. It was never enough to close school. But it was enough to interest Sam and Charlie. Especially because they were broke.

"I need money," said Sam at breakfast the next morning.

"Me, too. I don't know where all my money went," added Charlie.

"You bought a *snow*blower with it, you guys," said Kristy. "And you have not used it once. You have not cleared a single driveway."

Charlie looked glum. "I know. Sam and I are ready to work. If I used the snowblower and Sam used a shovel, we could

dig people out in no time. It's just that
. . ." Charlie paused.

"What?" I wanted to know.

"I hate calling people up and asking for
work."

"So do I," agreed Sam. "I am no good at
it."

"*I* could do that!" I cried. I jumped up
so fast I scared Boo-Boo. He went skittering
out of the kitchen. "I could call people. All
I would have to do is talk, and I am very
good at talking."

"Well, that is certainly true," said Kristy.

"Hannie and Nancy and I could *all* do
that," I went on. "I bet we could get you
lots of business."

"Really?" said Charlie. "Sam and I
would pay you part of what we earn every
time we shovel out a customer you find
for us."

"Oh, excellent! I will be rich!" I cried.
"We will all be rich! Now Sam, Charlie —
I need some information," I said impor-
tantly.

22

"What kind of information?" Sam looked puzzled.

"Oh, like how much you will charge your customers, and what time you will come to their houses to shovel them out. Oh, and the name of your business."

"Our name?" said Charlie. "Good point. What should we call ourselves?"

Charlie and Sam thought and thought. Finally Sam announced, "We will call ourselves the Thomas Brothers."

"The Thomas Brothers?" I repeated. That was pretty dull. "How about something more fun like . . . the Snowmen?"

Charlie shook his head. "Nope. We want to keep it plain and simple."

"All right. I will telephone Nancy and Hannie now. I will see if they want to help me."

I picked up the phone. I called my friends. They said they would be happy to find customers for Sam and Charlie. "They will do it!" I told my brothers.

"Great!" said Charlie. "Then it's a deal!"

That very day, the Three Musketeers found two customers for the Thomas Brothers. They were Hannie's family, and Mrs. Porter. Mrs. Porter lives next door to Daddy. I think she is a witch, but that is another story. Anyway, now she was a customer. The Thomas Brothers were in business.

Show and Share

On Sunday I helped Andrew and Emily make a snowman in the front yard. I was trying to be nice to my little brother since he was so confused about snow days. I even let him give the snowman his carrot nose. Then I let him name the snowman. Andrew said grandly, "His name is Bob."

On Sunday night when we were back at the little house, more snow fell. It fell softly in the darkness. When I looked out my window on Monday morning, there was a new

25

layer of snow on the bushes and the roof and the sidewalk and the street.

I felt very excited, but I knew better than to scream, "Snow day! Snow day!" We needed more than a few inches for a snow day. Instead, I turned on my radio. I listened to Dr. G. while I got dressed.

Suddenly I thought of something. The Thomas Brothers. They should be shoveling Hannie's driveway and sidewalk, and the witch's driveway and sidewalk. It didn't matter whether we had a snow day. Sam and Charlie had to shovel out their customers each time it snowed.

As soon as breakfast was over, I called the big house.

Sam answered the phone. "Hello, Thomas Brothers," he said.

"Hi, it's me, Karen. Did you and Charlie do your job this morning?"

"Yup. No problem," Sam replied. "We shoveled everyone out before breakfast. Mrs. Porter said we were prompt and tidy."

"Did you get paid?"

"Yes. And we have your money. Fifty cents from each customer. So that's a dollar for you and Hannie and Nancy. I don't know how you are going to split it."

"We will figure it out," I said.

I could not wait to tell Hannie and Nancy the news. When I did, Nancy said, "Yes!" and Hannie said, "Awesome!"

"Let's tell everyone about our new job at Show and Share today," I suggested. "This is a very good story."

I had trouble waiting for Show and Share. During reading, Ms. Colman had to say, "Karen, please do not talk to your neighbors." During math, Ricky Torres had to say, "Quit poking me, Karen." And twice I talked in class without raising my hand.

But *finally* Ms. Colman said, "Who has something for Show and Share?"

The Three Musketeers shot their hands in the air.

"Nancy?" said Ms. Colman.

"Hannie and Karen and I have something to share together," said Nancy.

28

Ms. Colman let us stand in front of the room. We stood in a row. I smiled at our audience. Then I said, "We have joined a business. Hannie and Nancy and I are, um . . ." (I was not sure what to call ourselves.)

"We are salespeople," said Hannie.

"That's right," said Nancy. "Salespeople. We sell snow shoveling."

"My brothers bought a snowblower," I explained. "We find customers for them and they shovel their driveways after it snows."

"They were shoveling this morning," added Hannie. "They pay us part of the money they earn. Today we earned a dollar."

"That is very creative, girls," said Ms. Colman.

I beamed. My teacher liked my idea! I almost said, "I thought of it all by myself." But I did not want to sound like a show-off. Instead I said, "This afternoon we are going to find some more customers."

"We are?" said Hannie.

"We are?" said Nancy.

"Sure," I replied. "Sam and Charlie finished their work easily today. They could shovel more driveways. And the more snow they shovel, the more money we earn."

"You sound like a good businesswoman, Karen," said Ms. Colman.

"Thank you," I replied.

An Invitation for Ms. Colman

All day long I felt so, so happy. Ms. Colman had said my snow shoveling idea was creative. And she had told me I was a good businesswoman. I could not wait to return to the little house that afternoon.

When I did, I ran straight to Mommy. She was in the kitchen with Andrew. "Mommy," I said. "I have to ask you —"

"Just a sec," she said. "Hold on." Mommy was sitting at the table. She was reading a booklet. A box was on the floor. Pieces to something were spread across the table.

"What is she doing?" I whispered to Andrew.

"She bought a special calculator today. She has to figure it out. She said the instructions are from Mars."

"What?" I said.

Mommy looked up then. "It's an electronic calculator and address book, honey. And I said the instructions sound like they were written by a Martian. They are impossible to follow."

"Oh. But Mommy, can — "

"In a minute, sweetie."

I left the kitchen then. When I went back later, the calculator and the booklet were still on the table. Mommy was trying to read the booklet and start dinner at the same time. Plus, Andrew was asking if he could fingerpaint. Mommy looked like she needed a nap.

Even so, I said, "Mommy, please may I ask you something?"

"Sure. What is it?" Mommy let out a sigh.

"Did you think about asking Ms. Colman

over for dinner? You said you would think about it. I know she would want to come."

"Mommy, are there really Martians?" asked Andrew at the same time.

The phone began to ring. Mommy reached for it.

"Please answer my question!" I yelped.

"Yes, you may invite Ms. Colman to dinner," said Mommy in a rush. Then she picked up the phone.

"All right!" I cried. "Thank you!" But Mommy was too busy to listen.

What a great day. I could invite my teacher over. My wonderful teacher who said I was a smart businesswoman with a creative idea.

"Oh!" I exclaimed. That reminded me.

As soon as Mommy had hung up the phone, I called Nancy. Then I called Hannie. "We have to get more customers."

Nancy had an idea. "How about the Kilbournes?" she suggested. The Kilbournes live next to Hannie and across from Daddy.

"Good idea," I replied. I called Mr. Kilbourne and he said he would be happy to hire the Thomas Brothers.

Then Hannie called the Kormans. They live on the other side of the Kilbournes. Melody Korman is our friend. Hannie told Mrs. Korman about the Thomas Brothers. And Mrs. Korman said, "Oh, what a life-saver. Just what we need. Will they come every time it snows?"

"Each and every time," Hannie told her. Then she phoned me with the news. She was very proud of herself.

"Excellent!" I said. "Four customers all together. Now you and Nancy and I will split *two* dollars every time it snows. I better call Sam and Charlie." So I did.

"Two more customers?" said Charlie. "That is great. I did not know you were lining up more business. But, hey! We can handle it. Thank you, Karen."

I did not know why Charlie was so surprised. I was just doing my job.

That night I went to bed thinking, More snow, more snow, please more snow!

Karen's Calendar

When I arrived at school the next day, I hung my coat in my cubby. Then I went straight to my desk and sat down. I did not fool around in the back of the room. I did not talk to Hannie or Nancy or Ricky or Natalie. I wanted to be on my best behavior when Ms. Colman came into the room.

"Good morning, Ms. Colman," I said politely as she put her things on her desk. "How are you today?"

"Just fine, thanks." My teacher smiled at me.

"Ms. Colman? Can you come over for dinner tonight?"

Ms. Colman paused. "Come over for dinner? Tonight?" she repeated. "Well, thank you. I would like to, but I am busy tonight."

"How about tomorrow night?" I asked.

"Karen, have you talked to your mother about this?" said Ms. Colman. "Does she know you are inviting me over for dinner?"

"Oh, yes," I replied. "She said I could ask you. She said so yesterday."

"Well, maybe you need to talk to her again. Then we can decide on a date. I need to plan ahead. My schedule is very busy right now."

"Okay."

Grown-ups always do things the hard way. When I want Nancy to come over, I call her and say, "Hey, Nancy, can you come over?" And most of the time she comes right over. Same with Hannie. But not with adults. Adults have to make Big Plans.

* * *

That afternoon I said to Mommy, "I hope you are not cooking anything extra. Ms. Colman cannot eat dinner with us tonight."

"Ms. Colman? You invited her over tonight?"

"Yes, but she cannot come. She cannot come tomorrow night, either. She said I should talk to you about a date."

"She's right. Karen, I'm sorry. I should have told you that yesterday. But I was so busy. I did not know you were going to invite Ms. Colman before we talked about it again. Let's look at my datebook right now."

Mommy got out her datebook. She kept flipping the pages back and forth. She and Seth are very busy people. Mommy had a hard time finding a free evening. But finally she chose a date. It was two weeks away.

"Two weeks!" I exclaimed. That seemed like forever. But it was worth waiting for.

I drew a red circle around that day on my own calendar.

Working Hard

The next morning Andrew woke me up. He stood by my bed in the dark and whispered, "Karen. It snowed again, Karen. Karen, look out the window."

More snow? I leaped out of bed. Andrew was right.

"I bet we got three inches!" I exclaimed.

"Is today a snow day?" asked Andrew.

"I do not think so. This is not enough snow." (Still, I turned on the radio to listen to Dr. G.) "But Sam and Charlie will be at work today," I told Andrew. "Now they have to shovel out four houses. I hope they got up early. I hope they know it snowed last night."

I almost telephoned the big house to make sure my brothers knew about the snow. Then I decided not to. Sometimes people tell me I am bossy. I did not want anyone to tell me that now. Also, I did not want to wake anyone up.

I waited until it was nearly time to leave for school. Then I called my brothers at the last minute.

"Did you finish all your work?" I asked Sam.

"Just barely," he replied. "We just barely made it. We will get to school on time if we skip breakfast. We worked *hard* this morning. I was not sure we were going to finish the Kormans' driveway."

Maybe you should get up earlier, I thought. But I did not say so. Sam and Charlie had done their job. That was all that mattered.

In school that morning I said to Nancy

and Hannie, "The Thomas Brothers owe us two more dollars today."

"I know," said Hannie. "I watched them working at our house. Charlie used the snowblower on the driveway and the sidewalk. Sam shoveled the path to our front door. Daddy says they are good workers."

"And we are good salespeople," I reminded my friends.

"Maybe we should get some more customers," said Nancy.

"Maybe," I replied.

When Ms. Colman entered our room, I left my friends. I ran to my teacher. "Guess what, Ms. Colman," I said. "I talked to Mommy and you can come to dinner two weeks from yesterday. Mommy looked in her datebook."

"Why, thank you, Karen," replied Ms. Colman. "Let me check *my* datebook."

Ms. Colman opened her purse. She pulled out a small book. She looked through the pages. "Uh-oh," she said a moment later. "I'm afraid I cannot make it that night, Karen. I'm . . . busy."

I think Ms. Colman blushed when she said that. But I hardly noticed.

"You cannot come?" I said. "But Mommy checked in her datebook. And I already marked my calendar. I drew a red circle around that day."

"Karen, I'm sorry. I think maybe your mother and I should look at our datebooks at the same time. We will find an evening that is good for everybody. These days I am a bit busier than usual."

She was? I wanted to know why, but I had a feeling I better not ask. This sounded like one of those grown-up things I am not supposed to ask a lot of questions about. So I just said, "Okay."

That afternoon, Mommy called Ms. Colman at school. She looked in her datebook while she talked to my teacher. Guess what. They found another evening when Mommy and Seth were free and so was Ms. Colman. And it was only two weeks from

Thursday. I would not have to wait *too* much longer.

I ran to my room and looked at my calendar again. I tried to erase the red circle I had made the day before. It would not come off. So I painted over it with Mommy's white-out. Then I drew a new red circle around two weeks from Thursday. Inside the circle I wrote *Dinner with Ms. Colman!* I hoped I could be patient about waiting for the big day.

Big News

I began a countdown to the big day. The countdown started with fifteen. Fifteen days until dinner with Ms. Colman. Fourteen days until dinner with Ms. Colman. Thirteen days, twelve days . . . eight days . . . five days. One Monday morning there were just three days left.

"Three days, three days!" I sang during breakfast. "Mommy, what are we going to eat for dinner on Thursday night?"

"What do you think Ms. Colman would like?" asked Mommy.

"Something special," I replied.

"Grilled monkey knuckles?" asked Seth.

"Not for my teacher!" I cried.

"Karen, I'm teasing."

"Let's have fish and salad. A salad with artichoke hearts in it," I suggested.

"That sounds delicious," said Mommy.

When school was over on Monday, I went straight to my room at the little house. I turned on my sound box to listen to Dr. G. I was getting to know Dr. G. pretty well. I listened to him every day.

"Big news!" announced Dr. G.

I sat up straight. I stared at the sound box, even though there was nothing to see. Dr. G. had never said, "Big news!" before.

"Something is brewing over the Great Lakes," Dr. G. went on. "It is heading our way. It should be a major snowstorm by the time it reaches us. Maybe not a blizzard, but one powerful storm. Watch for it in two or three days. And stayed tuned to WSTO for more details."

"Yes!" I cried. "Yes! Yes! Yes!"

I was so excited that I invited Hannie and Nancy over. When the Three Musketeers were together in my room I said, "I just know we are going to have a snow day. And I think we should make a snow day schedule. That way we will not forget to do a single fun snow thing."

We wrote out a schedule for an entire day. It started at 9:00 with "Build a snowman." It ended at 5:00 with "Ask Mommy for hot chocolate."

"There," I said. "We will have the best snow day ever."

Later, when my friends had gone home, I tuned into Dr. G. again. He was still predicting a gigundo snowstorm.

Big Storm

As soon as I woke up on Tuesday morning I turned on the radio. I waited for Dr. G. with the weather report.

"We are really going to get walloped," he said. "The storm is growing bigger and stronger. It will hit sometime tomorrow."

When Mommy came into my room, the first thing I said was, "What does 'walloped' mean?"

"Good morning, Karen," she replied.

"Good morning. What does 'walloped' mean?"

"It means 'hit hard.' Why?"

"Doctor G. said we will get walloped by the storm. Ooh, I cannot wait."

At school, everyone was talking about the storm.

"We might get a foot of snow," said Ricky.

"Remember the blizzard we had?" said Natalie. "Maybe the storm will turn into another blizzard."

We had a blizzard before Christmas. It was not even winter yet. It was still late autumn. But the snow did not know that. It came down hard, and the wind blew, and people got stranded. (Kristy's boyfriend got stranded at the big house. He spent the night in the guest room. Kristy was embarrassed.) We had a snow day then. I would have to remind Andrew about that, so he could figure out snow days.

The Three Musketeers huddled in the back of the classroom.

"A real storm! This is exciting," said Nancy.

"You know what?" said Hannie. "Now would be a good time to get some more customers for Sam and Charlie. Everyone will want their driveways shoveled after a huge storm."

"Hannie, that is a great idea!" I exclaimed. "Let's call some more people this afternoon. Can you guys come over to my house again?"

Hannie and Nancy both came to the little house after school. We sat at the table in the kitchen. I found a piece of paper and a pencil.

"Who should we call?" asked Nancy.

"People in my neighborhood," Hannie replied. "We should find jobs for Sam and Charlie that are nearby. We do not want them to waste time traveling all over town. Let's call other people on my street."

I made a list of neighbors to call. Hannie and Nancy and I took turns dialing the numbers. Each time we got a customer, I wrote down the address and phone number to give to my brothers. After we had lined up five new customers we decided we better stop.

"Sam and Charlie will be pretty busy," Nancy pointed out.

"Boy, it sure was easy to get more customers," I said.

"Nobody wants to shovel their driveway after a huge storm," added Hannie.

When Hannie and Nancy had gone home, I called the big house. I had to tell Sam and Charlie what the Three Musketeers had done that afternoon.

But no one answered the telephone.

I decided to go to my room and listen to Dr. G. Maybe he had more news. Maybe the storm had turned into a blizzard. While I waited for Dr. G.'s report I listened to four songs. I danced around the room with the microphone. When the last song ended, I bowed to Emily Junior and Goosie. "Thank you. Thank you, lady and gentleman," I said.

Then I heard Dr. G.'s voice on the radio. "The storm is on its way. It should hit

our area sometime tomorrow. Expect anywhere from eight to twelve inches of snow,
folks."

Ooh, I was ready for the storm. I could
not wait for tomorrow.

Leaving School

When I woke up on Wednesday morning, light snow was already falling. It was so light and fine it was hard to see. But it was falling, all right. In a flash I turned on my sound box. I had not expected snow so early. Maybe school would be closed today *and* tomorrow. It would be a shame if we were snowed in while we were *at* school. That would not be any fun. It would probably not even count as a snow day.

Dr. G. said, "Bundle up, folks! The storm

is coming." But he did not say a single thing about school closing.

So I got dressed.

By the time Seth was driving Nancy and me through town, the snow was falling a little harder. The street was turning white.

"Seth, what if we get stuck at school?" I asked.

"I do not think that will happen," he replied.

"But what if it does?"

"Then I will come and rescue you. I will save the day."

I giggled. " 'Bye, Seth!" I called, when he stopped in front of our school.

That morning, Ms. Colman said, "The storm is coming, class."

I raised my hand. "That is what Doctor G. said on the radio today," I announced. "And he said eight to twelve inches of snow."

"Thank you, Karen," Ms. Colman replied. "That is just why I thought today would be perfect for our snow unit. We are going to study snow crystals. What have we already learned about snow crystals?"

Bobby Gianelli waved his hand around until Ms. Colman called on him. "No two crystals are ever the same," he said. "Each one is different from every other crystal in the entire world. And from every other snowflake that has ever, ever fallen, or ever will fall."

Well, for heaven's sake. Bobby was right, of course. But usually he does not give such long answers.

Anyway, while the snow fell outside, my friends and I looked at pictures of snow crystals. We looked at some books about crystals that Ms. Colman had taken out of our school library. Then Ms. Colman let us go into the courtyard outside of our classroom. We tried to collect real snowflakes so we could look at them under microscopes. This was hard. The flakes kept melting. But I saw three, and they really were different from each other.

By lunchtime the snow was piling up in

the courtyard. The wind was beginning to blow, and it swirled the flakes around. My friends and I kept looking out the window. After lunch, we got a little bit noisy. Nobody could sit still. Ms. Colman let us cut out paper snowflakes and tack them onto the bulletin board.

The sky grew dark and the snow fell harder. And then a voice came over the intercom in our classroom. "May I have your attention, please?" said our principal. "Due to the storm, school will close early today. Buses will be arriving shortly. Your parents have been notified. Please get ready to leave as quickly as possible."

I turned to look at Ricky. Ooh, that storm must be big!

Mrs. Dawes picked up Nancy and me and drove us home. She had to drive very slowly. Once the car went wiggling across the road. Mrs. Dawes said she was glad she did not live in Alaska.

When we reached Nancy's house, I called, "Thank you, Mrs. Dawes! 'Bye,

Nancy! Remember our snow day schedule for tomorrow!" Then I ran to Mommy's. I did not bother to listen to Dr. G. that afternoon. The storm had arrived. I knew school would be closed the next day. Thursday would be great. The Thomas Brothers would earn money for the Three Musketeers, my friends and I would play in the snow, and Ms. Colman would come for dinner.

Karen's Snow Day

That night I was too excited to fall asleep.

"Bedtime, Karen!" called Mommy.

"Okay," I replied. But when she and Seth came into my room, I was jumping up and down on my bed. "I *love* storms!" I announced.

"Settle down, honey," said Seth.

I tried to. But after I turned out my light, I kept sitting up to look out the window. Once, the snow was coming down so hard I could not even see the house across the street.

58

I woke up early on Thursday morning. I tuned into Dr. G. I knew school would be closed, but I wanted to hear Dr. G. say so himself. When he said, "In Stoneybrook, all public, private, and parochial schools are closed," I cheered. "Yea! Hooray!"

Andrew ran into my room. "Is today a snow day, Karen?" he asked.

"Yes," I replied. "Today is a snow day. School is closed because we got so much snow." (In fact, it was still snowing.) "Just like the blizzard. Remember that, Andrew?"

He nodded. Then he said, "Well, let's go make a snowman."

"Andrew, it is still dark outside. We have to wait."

While we waited, we went downstairs. I found the snow day schedule that the Three Musketeers had made. I hoped Hannie would be able to get to the little house. The snow day would not be as much fun without her. The Three Musketeers were supposed to be together. But the roads were still covered with snow. The plows had not come through town yet. Maybe they would not come until the snow stopped. I wondered if I should call Hannie. No, it was too early.

But then the phone rang. Maybe Hannie was calling me!

I raced for the phone. "Hello?" I said.

"Hello, is this Karen?"

I did not recognize the voice, so all I replied was, "Who is calling, please?"

"This is Mr. Hsu."

Mr. Hsu. He lives down the street from Daddy. "Oh, hi. This is Karen," I said.

"Hi. I was wondering where your brothers are," said Mr. Hsu. "They have not arrived yet. They are supposed to shovel our driveway."

I looked at the clock in the kitchen. "Well, it is still very early," I told Mr. Hsu. "They will be there soon."

As soon as I hung up, the phone rang again. This time Mrs. Meyer was calling. She asked about Sam and Charlie, too.

Hmm. I thought back to Tuesday when Hannie and Nancy and I found the new customers for the Thomas Brothers. Had I remembered to tell Sam and Charlie about that? I had called them, and no one had answered the phone, and then . . . I had never called back.

Uh-oh.

I looked outside. Daylight. The night was over. Snow was still falling, but not as hard as on the day before. Sam and Charlie were probably outside already. I would not even reach them if I called the big house. But I would have to try anyway. Kristy or someone would have to tell my brothers what I had done. They had to shovel out five more driveways, and they did not even know it.

I dialed the number at Daddy's house. Sam answered the phone.

"Sam!" I exclaimed. "I did not think you would be at home."

"Hi, Karen," said Sam. "I just came back for a pair of dry gloves."

"Um, Sam?" I began. I told him about the new customers.

"Karen! I cannot believe you did this. How could you forget to call Charlie and me? And besides, it will take us forever to shovel out all those people."

"Well, you do have all day to work," I pointed out. "No school."

"And you are going to help us," replied Sam.

The Thomas Brothers and the Three Musketeers

I did not like the sound of that. What had Sam meant when he said, "And you are going to help us"? It was a snow day. I had waited for it for weeks. I had made plans. I had a snow day schedule.

"You stay right by the phone, Karen," said Sam. "I am going to talk to Charlie. Then I will call you back."

Boo. Sam was mad at me. Charlie would probably be mad, too. And then maybe Hannie and Nancy would be mad when they heard what was happening to our snow day.

Fifteen minutes later Sam called back. "Karen, you have to come help us. Charlie is going to borrow Mr. Korman's truck. It has four-wheel drive." (I did not know what four-wheel drive was, but I did not bother to ask.) "He is going to drive over to your house and bring you back here. Then you are going to help us today."

"Okay," I said. " 'Bye."

I told Mommy and Seth what had happened. Then I called Nancy and Hannie. We decided that Nancy should go over to the big house with me. Maybe the Three Musketeers could have their snow day together at Daddy's instead of Mommy's. (Part of the snow day, anyway.)

When Charlie arrived at the little house, he was grumpy. Nancy and I tried not to notice. We were bundled up in our snow day clothes — layers and layers of sweaters and scarves and hats and gloves and mittens and jackets. Nancy was even wearing

64

plastic bags inside her boots. She said they kept her feet extra dry.

"Hi, Charlie!" I called as Nancy and I climbed into the truck. We squished together in the cab next to him.

"Hi," he answered. After a pause, he added, "Nice of you to let me know we have nine customers now, instead of four."

"I *said* I was sorry."

"I am sorry, too," added Nancy.

"Karen, don't you know that on school mornings, Sam and I would never have enough time to shovel out nine driveways?"

"Oops," said Nancy and I.

"After today we will have to get rid of the five new customers."

"Okay."

Charlie did not say another word until we reached the big house. The ride through town was slow and slippery. Charlie tried to drive on streets that had already been plowed. Even so, that truck just crept along like a sleepy turtle.

Hannie was waiting for us at Daddy's.

She was standing in the yard in her snow-suit, waving and smiling. At least my friends were not mad at me. Nancy and I waded through the snow to Hannie. "We just have to help Sam and Charlie a little," I told her. "Then we can start our snow day. I even remembered to bring our schedule with me. It is in my pocket."

The Thomas Brothers and the Three Musketeers sat in the kitchen at the big house. "First," said Charlie, "Sam and I need a list of the new customers. Then we need you to find all the dry gloves and mittens you can. Ours keep getting soaked."

"Also," said Sam, "we have already shoveled out Mrs. Porter's house and Hannie's house, and we are in the middle of work over at the Kilbournes'. Karen, you guys better call the other customers and tell them we will get to their houses later than you said. And tell the new people you have to cancel their service after today."

I sighed. By the time we did all that, the morning would be half gone.

The Snowman

I was right. Nancy and Hannie and I could not even look at our snow day schedule until after eleven o'clock.

"But the schedule started at nine!" cried Nancy.

"We have missed two hours," added Hannie.

"I know," I said. I felt horrible since this was my fault. "Well, let's see. We could skip the first two hours of the schedule — "

"No!" exclaimed Hannie. "Then we do not get to build a snowman."

"You want to build a snowman?" I asked.

"Yes," replied my friends.

"Well . . . then let's go!" I said.

We put on our layers of clothes again. We wasted a little time searching for plastic bags. Hannie and I wanted our feet to look just like Nancy's. When we were as bundled up as could be, we went outside. (We could not move very fast.) We stood in the front yard.

"Look at all the snow," I said.

"It is very beautiful," said Nancy.

Snow covered the neighborhood. It was piled on the roofs of the houses. It dripped off every branch of every tree. A sea of snow.

"I wish it would snow every night," said Hannie.

My friends and I tramped across the yard. We had to lift our feet high. From down the street came the sound of the snowblower. I could see Charlie clearing a driveway. Nearby, Sam was using a shovel to clear a sidewalk. I waved to Sam but he did not see me.

Hannie and Nancy and I packed a big snowball. Then we began to roll it around the yard. After a few minutes, Hannie yelled, "Okay, stop! This is the perfect size for the snowman's head."

We put the head by a tree.

"Now let's start his middle," said Nancy.

But we did not have a chance. Sam came trudging into the yard then. "We need gloves and change," he announced.

"Change?" I repeated.

"For the Hsus. They could not pay us the exact amount of money. Do you have four quarters for a dollar?"

"I don't know," I said. "I will have to check. I will get you the gloves for now. Then we will look for change."

I ran inside and got two pairs of dry gloves. I gave them to Sam. "I still do not know about the change," I said. "You better go back to work. Give me the dollar. When I get four quarters I will bring them to you."

The Three Musketeers had to stop work-

ing on the snowman. We left his head by the tree and went inside. I looked in my piggy bank. "Nope," I said, shaking my head. "I only have sixty-two cents."

"That's all?" said Hannie.

"The rest is at the little house, in my other bank." What a pain.

"How about you, Hannie?" asked Nancy.

"I have two dollars at home," she replied. "But they are bills."

Well, that was no help.

Kristy had three quarters.

"Give Sam one of your quarters, plus Kristy's three," suggested Nancy.

"Who do I give the dollar to?" I asked.

We kept asking people for money. Finally Elizabeth said she had four quarters. We gave her the dollar and ran outside with the change for Sam.

"Thanks," he said. "Just in time."

The Three Musketeers went back to my house. We looked at the poor, lonely snowman's head. But we decided not to finish him. We were just too tired.

The Picnic in
the Living Room

"Karen, what time is it?" asked Nancy.

The Three Musketeers had just come back from giving Sam the quarters. We were taking off our wet clothes (again). I felt as if I had spent half the day putting on and taking off my snow clothes.

I looked at my watch. "Uh-oh. It is after twelve-thirty!" I said.

"The morning is over," added Hannie, "and we did not even finish the snowman. Our schedule is no good now."

"Anyway, Sam and Charlie are still working. I bet they will need us to help them some more," I said. "I have a feeling we are not done working."

"Girls?" said Elizabeth when we went into the kitchen.

"Yeah?" I replied. I knew I did not look happy or sound happy.

"I'm sorry you cannot follow your snow day schedule. I know you were looking forward to that," said Elizabeth.

I nodded. "Thank you."

"I also know you did not mean to cause any trouble for Sam and Charlie. You were just trying to do your job."

"That's right," I said.

"But we do have to help Sam and Charlie," added Nancy.

"That is our duty," spoke up Hannie.

"Well, how about taking a little break," said Elizabeth. She was smiling. "How would you like to come to a picnic in the living room?"

"Sure!" exclaimed Hannie. "But what is a picnic in the living room?"

74

"Just what it sounds like. You can eat lunch on the floor by the fireplace. I will see if anyone else wants to come."

Elizabeth invited everyone at the big house to the picnic. And everyone came except for Sam and Charlie. They said they could not take a break, even though they were starving.

Nannie spread a yellow checkered tablecloth on the floor by the fireplace. Earlier, Kristy had built a big fire. We all helped carry things into the living room: plastic bowls, soup spoons, paper cups, and napkins. Daddy and Elizabeth carried in a plate of sandwiches, a pot of soup, and a thermos of hot chocolate.

Nancy and Hannie and I played Lovely Ladies.

"Mmm, this hot chocolate is delectable," I said.

"Scrumptious," said Nancy.

"Everyone raise your pinkies," added Hannie.

I had so much fun at the Lovely Ladies

luncheon in the living room that I almost forgot about the Thomas Brothers and the ruined snow day. In fact, I said, "Hey, let's go finish our snowman, okay?"

"His head has been buried in a snow-drift," Hannie told me.

"Then we will just start over again," I replied. "Let's not waste another second."

The Three Musketeers helped clean up the picnic. We put on our snow clothes again. We were stamping our feet into our boots when Charlie banged through the back door.

"Oh, there you are," he said to my friends and me. "I need more gas for the snowblower. And Sam and I decided to eat on the job. Could you and your friends bring us some lunch?"

Oh, no. Not again. We would *never* finish our poor snowman. I sighed loudly.

Elizabeth helped Hannie and Nancy fix some food for the Thomas Brothers. I went out to the garage with Charlie. I helped him look for the gasoline can. After the boys got their lunch and the gas, they said they needed dry gloves again. Then they wanted hot chocolate.

The Three Musketeers gave up on the snowman.

A Bad End to
a Bad Day

At three-thirty that afternoon Hannie and Nancy and I were standing in my front yard again.

"Does anyone feel like playing?" asked Hannie.

"There is no point," I answered. "Here comes Sam again."

"I wonder what he wants this time," said Nancy.

So I yelled, "What do you want, Sam?"

Sam was trudging along the sidewalk. He was carrying his shovel. "Nothing," he replied. "Charlie and I are finished. Mr. Meyer is paying Charlie. At least we earned a lot of money today."

"Hey, so did we!" I cried. I had almost forgotten about that.

"How much?" Hannie wanted to know.

"Let's see," said Sam. "Nine people times fifty cents. That's four dollars and fifty cents. So for each of you , that is . . ."

"I think it is a dollar-fifty," said Nancy.

"A dollar-fifty!" I exclaimed. "For all that work? And for missing our snow day? Bull-frogs. That is not enough."

"Well, this will not happen again. Will it, Karen?" said Sam.

"No. I called the five new people just like you told me to. They know you can-not work for them anymore," I re-plied.

"Good."

"Well, we are done. Finally," called Charlie. He was lugging the snowblower along the sidewalk.

"Charlie? Are you still mad at me?" I asked in a small voice.

"No." Charlie even smiled at my friends and me. "You guys were a big help today. Thank you. And Sam and I earned a ton of money. Oh, by the way, I have your share." Charlie gave each of us a one-dollar bill and two quarters.

I looked at Hannie and Nancy. "We wasted the whole snow day," I said. I almost began to cry.

"Not the *whole* day," Charlie pointed out. "You could still build a fort or something."

"I am too tired to build anything," said Nancy.

"Me, too," said Hannie and I.

"Well, maybe we will have another snow day soon," said Sam.

"Maybe," I replied. But I did not really think so.

"Save the schedule, just in case," added Hannie.

The Thomas Brothers and the Three Musketeers went inside. We started to peel off

our wet clothes for about the one hun-
dredth time.

"Wait!" cried Charlie. "Karen, when do
you and Nancy want to leave? If you leave
now, you will not have to take off your
things again."

"Then let's leave now," I said. So Nancy
and I called good-bye to Hannie. Then I
said good-bye to my big-house family. And
then Charlie drove Nancy and me home in
his old car, the Junk Bucket.

"You still have one thing to look forward
to," said Nancy on the way. "Dinner with
Ms. Colman."

"Oh! That's right! She is coming at six
o'clock!" I exclaimed.

But guess what happened when I
reached the little house. Mommy met me
at the door.

"Honey, Ms. Colman just telephoned,"
she said. (Uh-oh. I had a bad feeling about
that.) "She will not be able to come over
tonight. The roads where she lives have not
been plowed yet. Her house is way out in

the country, remember? So we will have to find another evening for our dinner."

Boo.

Boo, boo, boo, and bullfrogs.

It had been a horrible day. The worst snow day ever.

Surprise!

"Good morning! Good morning!" said Dr. G.

"Oh, be quiet," I replied.

It was Friday morning. Our snow day was over. My radio alarm had turned itself on. It was time to get up. (Really, I do not think it is fair that I have to wake up when it is still dark outside.)

I slapped at my radio to turn it off. I yawned. I sat up in bed. Lazily I pulled up my window shade and peeked outside.

It was snowing again! It was really and

truly snowing! I could not believe it. Yea, hurray! Two snow days in a row!

"Mommy! Mommy!" I shrieked. "Seth! Andrew! It is snowing!"

Mommy and Seth hurried to my room. They were rubbing their eyes. "Honey?" said Mommy sleepily. "What's wrong?"

"It is snowing! Look outside!"

Mommy and Seth looked out my window.

"I think it is just a flurry," said Seth. "It is not snowing hard."

"And Karen, please do not wake up the entire household every time it snows," added Mommy. "You are forgetting your indoor voice."

Well, boo and bullfrogs. Mommy was no fun. Neither was Seth.

"Sorry," I said.

Mommy and Seth went back to their room. I started to get into bed again. But Mommy called over her shoulder, "Time to dress for school, Karen."

"Okay," I answered. I looked out my

window again. It was still snowing, so I turned Dr. G. on. When it was time for the next weather report, I said, "I am sorry I told you to be quiet, Doctor G." Then I listened to him carefully.

"Today will be sunny and bright," he announced. "The storm has moved out to sea. Temperatures will hover right around thirty degrees. Here in Stoneybrook, all roads have been plowed and all schools will be open."

"Look outside!" I exclaimed. "It is snowing!" (I remembered to whisper loudly instead of yelling.)

"You may see a passing flurry early this morning," Dr. G. added. "But by nine o'clock, the skies will be clear."

"Darn!" I said.

I pouted. I made faces. I turned off old Dr. G. again. What did he know? After I got dressed, I stomped into the bathroom. Then I stomped around looking for my workbooks to take to school. Then I

stomped downstairs to breakfast. I flumped
into my chair.

"Karen, what on earth is the matter?"
asked Mommy.

"I did not get my snow day, and Ms.
Colman did not come to dinner. That is
what is the matter," I replied.

The phone rang then and Mommy answered it. She listened for a few moments.
She smiled. Then she said thank you and
hung up. She was still smiling. "Well,
Karen," she said, "I think you just got your
snow day. That was someone from school.
Stoneybrook Academy is closed today. The
boiler is broken. You cannot go back to
school until Monday."

I jumped to my feet. "Really? I do not
believe it!"

"Really," said Mommy. "There is no heat
at your school."

"But today is not a real snow day," said
Andrew. He looked confused. "Karen told
me about snow days. And this is not one."

"Oh, I don't care!" I cried. "It is a day

off from school, and we have *tons* of snow, and I still have the snow day schedule. Mommy, can I invite Hannie and Nancy over for the whole day? We have a lot to do."

"Okay," said Mommy. "Go ahead."

"Thank you." I picked up the phone and dialed my two best friends.

Angels and Ice Skates

"Hannie! Hannie!" I cried, when Hannie answered the telephone. "Did you hear the news about our school?"

"Yes! The boiler is broken!"

"And you know what that means? It means we can have our snow day after all. Mommy said so. Can you come over right away? The roads are clear. Oh, and bring your ice skates."

I called Nancy and said the same things to her. She ran to my house as soon as we hung up the phone. Hannie's mother

dropped her off about twenty minutes later. It was nine o'clock on the dot.

"Perfect," I said. "This is just when our snow day begins. All right. Now we can really build a snowman."

The Three Musketeers went outside. We had the entire yard to ourselves. Even Andrew was not around. He was at his preschool. We decided to build a snowman and a snowwoman. (We named them Dudley and Fiona.) We gave them lots of dress-up clothes because they were on their way to a ball.

When Dudley and Fiona were finished we flopped on the ground. We made a herd of snow angels, one after the other. Do you know how to make a snow angel? It is gigundoly easy. You lie on your back in the snow and sweep your arms up to your head, then down to your sides. Then you sweep your legs apart and together, apart and together. And then you stand up very carefully. In the snow you can see the angel's head and body and wings and skirt.

"Let's decorate the angels," I said. We made very fancy clothes for them with food coloring. *Squirt, squirt, squirt.*

When the angels were finished we made a snow fort.

"But we cannot have a fight," said Nancy. "There are three of us. That would be two against one, and two against one is no fair."

We decided our snow fort was a snow playhouse instead. We held an outdoor tea party in it. (Even though our schedule said "Snowball fight.")

"Guess what," said Hannie when the tea party was over. "I am all soaky and wet. I need to go inside for awhile."

"Me, too," said Nancy.

"Well, anyway, it is lunchtime," I told my friends.

The Three Musketeers hung their wet clothes in the kitchen. Andrew had come home from preschool by then, and he watched us.

"What is the proper lunch for a snow

day?" Mommy wanted to know.

I looked at the schedule. "Alphabet soup, peanut butter and honey sandwiches, and milk," I announced.

"Can I eat with you?" asked Andrew.

"I guess," I replied. Andrew is a pain when he eats alphabet soup. He keeps borrowing letters out of other people's bowls. He is not happy until he has spelled the name of every person at the table.

But Andrew was not too bad during lunch that day. So we let him ice skate with us. We make a skating rink every year by filling our wading pool with water. Then we let the water freeze and we can skate around.

By five o'clock Andrew and my friends and I were very tired. But we were happy, too. I got a good idea.

"Mommy," I said, "let's just *see* if maybe Ms. Colman could come to dinner tonight. She had the day off, too. And all the roads have been plowed."

"All right," said Mommy. "Good idea."

94

Mommy called Ms. Colman at her house. She invited her to dinner. I watched Mommy's face carefully. She began to smile, so I did, too. When she hung up the phone she said, "Ms. Colman will be here at seven o'clock."

Ms. Colman's
Wonderful News

"Mommy, everything has to be perfect for Ms. Colman," I said. I looked at my watch. Five-thirty. Hannie and Nancy had gone home. Ms. Colman would ring our doorbell in just one hour and a half.

"Why don't you set the table?" suggested Mommy. "You may put out any china you want. And maybe you could make a center-piece."

"Oh! I will make placecards, too. Thank you, Mommy."

I decided to set the table with our very

best china. It is the china we use on special occasions, like Thanksgiving. While I was doing that, I said, "Mommy, what are we going to have for dinner? We did not know Ms. Colman would be coming *this* night."

"I know," replied Mommy. "But I can still fix fish and salad, just like you wanted. I do not have any dessert, though."

"May I make dessert?" I asked. "We can have Jello-O pudding. I know how to make that. I made it at the big house."

"Okay," said Mommy.

Goodness. I was very busy. After I set the table I made a centerpiece. I put a bowl of fruit in the middle of the table. Around it I put candles in brass holders. I tied red ribbons to the holders.

Then I made the placecards. Andrew wanted to help me, but I would not let him. He does not stay in the lines when he colors. Besides, I had already let him be a pest when my friends and I were eating alphabet soup.

"Can't I do *some*thing?" begged Andrew.

I gave Andrew the placecards when they were finished and told him where to put each one. Then we stood back and admired the table. It looked very beautiful.

Next I made the Jell-O pudding and Andrew helped me. After that we got dressed up in our most gorgeous holiday clothes. Also, I cleaned up my room.

At six o'clock Seth came home. At six-thirty Nancy called to find out what we were serving Ms. Colman for dinner. (She thought chocolate pudding was a nice dessert idea.) At seven o'clock the doorbell rang.

I froze. Then I whispered. "That is my teacher. Ms. Colman is here."

"Answer the door!" cried Andrew. He was jumping up and down.

I walked to the door very primly, like a Lovely Lady. I opened it slowly and said, "Good evening, Ms. Colman. Won't you come in?"

"Why, thank you, Karen," said Ms. Colman.

Seth hung up Ms. Colman's coat. The grown-ups sat in the living room and talked for a while. I did not know what to say. But then Ms. Colman said, "Karen, would you show me your room? I would love to see it."

"Sure!" I exclaimed. I took Ms. Colman's hand. I led her upstairs. "This is it," I said when we were standing in the doorway. "My room." (I was glad I had cleaned it up.) I showed Ms. Colman everything. "This is Goosie, and this is Tickly, and there is Emily Junior in her cage. There is where I keep my glasses when I am not wearing them. Oh, and here come Rocky and Midgie."

After the tour of my room we ate dinner. Ms. Colman said she liked the fish and salad very much. She cleaned her plate, so I know she really meant it. Then I served dessert. "I made this myself," I said.

While we were eating the chocolate Jell-O pudding, Ms. Colman made a Surprising Announcement. She makes them all

100

the time in school. I did not know she made them in dining rooms, too.

"I am engaged to be married," said Ms. Colman. "That is why I have been so busy lately. The wedding will be several months from now. After the wedding I will go away for awhile for our honeymoon. But then I will come back to school. Oh, and my name will still be Ms. Colman."

"Yea!" I cried.

"Congratulations!" said Mommy and Seth.

I got up from the table and gave my teacher a hug. This was exciting news. It was the perfect way to end the best snow day ever.

About the Author

ANN M. MARTIN lives in New York City and loves animals, especially cats. She has two cats of her own, Mouse and Rosie.

Other books by Ann M. Martin that you might enjoy are *Stage Fright*; *Me and Katie (the Pest)*; and the books in *The Baby-sitters Club* series.

Ann likes ice cream and *I Love Lucy*. And she has her own little sister, whose name is Jane.

Little Sister

Don't miss #35

KAREN'S DOLL HOSPITAL

Hannie and Nancy and I filled up three pillowcases with dolls and stuffed animals, too. We brought them all back to my room.

"Make yourselves at home," I said. "I am sure Hyacynthia will be glad to see you when she wakes up."

"Oh, look," said Hannie. "My Doll Sister, Kerry, has a scratch on her cheek."

"Poor Kerry!" said Nancy. "I hope Pokey didn't scratch her." (Pokey is Nancy's mischievous kitten.)

"This is perfect," I said. "We will open a doll hospital here while Hyacynthia is getting better. She will have lots of company. We can pretend we are doll doctors!"

LITTLE APPLE®

BABY SITTERS
Little Sister™

by Ann M. Martin,
author of The Baby-sitters Club ®

☐	MQ44300-3	#1	Karen's Witch	$2.95
☐	MQ44259-7	#2	Karen's Roller Skates	$2.95
☐	MQ44299-7	#3	Karen's Worst Day	$2.95
☐	MQ44264-3	#4	Karen's Kittycat Club	$2.95
☐	MQ44258-9	#5	Karen's School Picture	$2.95
☐	MQ44298-8	#6	Karen's Little Sister	$2.95
☐	MQ44257-0	#7	Karen's Birthday	$2.95
☐	MQ42670-2	#8	Karen's Haircut	$2.95
☐	MQ43652-X	#9	Karen's Sleepover	$2.95
☐	MQ43651-1	#10	Karen's Grandmothers	$2.95
☐	MQ43650-3	#11	Karen's Prize	$2.95
☐	MQ43649-X	#12	Karen's Ghost	$2.95
☐	MQ43648-1	#13	Karen's Surprise	$2.95
☐	MQ43646-5	#14	Karen's New Year	$2.95
☐	MQ43645-7	#15	Karen's in Love	$2.95
☐	MQ43644-9	#16	Karen's Goldfish	$2.95
☐	MQ43643-0	#17	Karen's Brothers	$2.95
☐	MQ43642-2	#18	Karen's Home-Run	$2.75
☐	MQ43641-4	#19	Karen's Good-Bye	$2.95
☐	MQ44823-4	#20	Karen's Carnival	$2.95
☐	MQ44824-2	#21	Karen's New Teacher	$2.95
☐	MQ44833-1	#22	Karen's Little Witch	$2.95
☐	MQ44832-3	#23	Karen's Doll	$2.95
☐	MQ44859-5	#24	Karen's School Trip	$2.95
☐	MQ44831-5	#25	Karen's Pen Pal	$2.95
☐	MQ44830-7	#26	Karen's Ducklings	$2.95
☐	MQ44829-3	#27	Karen's Big Joke	$2.95
☐	MQ44828-5	#28	Karen's Tea Party	$2.95
☐	MQ44825-0	#29	Karen's Cartwheel	$2.75
☐	MQ45645-8	#30	Karen's Kittens	$2.95
☐	MQ45646-6	#31	Karen's Bully	$2.95
☐	MQ45647-4	#32	Karen's Pumpkin Patch	$2.95
☐	MQ45648-2	#33	Karen's Secret	$2.95
☐	MQ45650-4	#34	Karen's Snow Day	$2.95
☐	MQ45652-0	#35	Karen's Doll Hospital	$2.95
☐	MQ45651-2	#36	Karen's New Friend	$2.95
☐	MQ45653-9	#37	Karen's Tuba	$2.95
☐	MQ45655-5	#38	Karen's Big Lie	$2.95
☐	MQ45654-7	#39	Karen's Wedding	$2.95
☐	MQ47040-X	#40	Karen's Newspaper	$2.95
☐	MQ47041-8	#41	Karen's School	$2.95
☐	MQ47042-6	#42	Karen's Pizza Party	$2.95
☐	MQ46912-6	#43	Karen's Toothache	$2.95

More Titles... ➡

💜 The Baby-sitters Little Sister titles continued...

☐	MQ47043-4	#44	Karen's Big Weekend	$2.95
☐	MQ47044-2	#45	Karen's Twin	$2.95
☐	MQ47045-0	#46	Karen's Baby-sitter	$2.95
☐	MQ46913-4	#47	Karen's Kite	$2.95
☐	MQ47046-9	#48	Karen's Two Families	$2.95
☐	MQ47047-7	#49	Karen's Stepmother	$2.95
☐	MQ47048-5	#50	Karen's Lucky Penny	$2.95
☐	MQ48229-7	#51	Karen's Big Top	$2.95
☐	MQ48299-8	#52	Karen's Mermaid	$2.95
☐	MQ48300-5	#53	Karen's School Bus	$2.95
☐	MQ48301-3	#54	Karen's Candy	$2.95
☐	MQ48230-0	#55	Karen's Magician	$2.95
☐	MQ48302-1	#56	Karen's Ice Skates	$2.95
☐	MQ48303-X	#57	Karen's School Mystery	$2.95
☐	MQ48304-8	#58	Karen's Ski Trip	$2.95
☐	MQ48231-9	#59	Karen's Leprechaun	$2.95
☐	MQ48305-6	#60	Karen's Pony	$2.95
☐	MQ48306-4	#61	Karen's Tattletale	$2.95
☐	MQ49307-2	#62	Karen's New Bike	$2.95
☐	MQ25996-2	#63	Karen's Movie	$2.95
☐	MQ25997-0	#64	Karen's Lemonade Stand	$2.95
☐	MQ25998-9	#65	Karen's Toys	$2.95
☐	MQ26279-3	#66	Karen's Monsters	$2.95
☐	MQ26024-3	#67	Karen's Turkey Day	$2.95
☐	MQ26025-1	#68	Karen's Angel	$2.95
☐	MQ26193-2	#69	Karen's Big Sister	$2.95
☐	MQ26280-7	#70	Karen's Grandad	$2.95
☐	MQ26194-0	#71	Karen's Island Adventure	$2.95
☐	MQ26195-9	#72	Karen's New Puppy	$2.95
☐	MQ55407-7		BSLS Jump Rope Rhymes Pack	$5.99
☐	MQ47677-7		BSLS School Scrapbook	$2.95
☐	MQ43647-3		Karen's Wish Super Special #1	$3.25
☐	MQ44834-X		Karen's Plane Trip Super Special #2	$3.25
☐	MQ44827-7		Karen's Mystery Super Special #3	$3.25
☐	MQ45644-X		Karen, Hannie, and Nancy — The Three Musketeers Super Special #4	$2.95
☐	MQ45649-0		Karen's Baby Super Special #5	$3.50
☐	MQ46911-8		Karen's Campout Super Special #6	$3.25

Available wherever you buy books, or use this order form.

Scholastic Inc., P.O. Box 7502, 2931 E. McCarty Street, Jefferson City, MO 65102

Please send me the books I have checked above. I am enclosing $ _____
(please add $2.00 to cover shipping and handling). Send check or money order – no
cash or C.O.Ds please.

Name _____ Birthdate _____

Address _____

City _____ State/Zip _____

Please allow four to six weeks for delivery. Offer good in U.S.A. only. Sorry, mail orders are not
available to residents to Canada. Prices subject to change.   BLS995